Elizabeth Mayhew Edmonds

Hesperas

Rhythm and Rhyme

Elizabeth Mayhew Edmonds

Hesperas
Rhythm and Rhyme

ISBN/EAN: 9783337271794

Printed in Europe, USA, Canada, Australia, Japan

Cover: Foto ©Andreas Hilbeck / pixelio.de

More available books at **www.hansebooks.com**

HESPERAS

HESPERAS

RHYTHM AND RHYME

BY

E. M. EDMONDS

LONDON

KEGAN PAUL, TRENCH & CO., 1, PATERNOSTER SQUARE.

1883

CONTENTS.

———◇◇———

SONNETS.

HESPĒRAS.

HESPĒRAS—in the evening, 'neath the arch
Of thick leaves soft stirred by the western wind
Where the last gold ray lights the dusky larch,
And trembles through the beech' arms low in
    clined,—
Between the pauses of the throstle's song,
Between the interchange of loving thought,
In simple rhymes some inner feelings strong,
I bring to 'guile the hour (yet not unsought) ;
While, circling round, the blithe bat's filmy wing
With quick erratic motion fan the face,
In eager hasting, ere swift darkness brings
The time to seek its shrouded nesting-place.

B

When Love is speaking, Love will listen long ;
And deep-browed night its dew-damp cloak hath
        donned
Full oft, whilst my dull pipe its crudest song,
To ears indulgent of its sounds, prolonged.

II.

Hespēras—in the evening, whilst the flame
From crackling logs threw out a sparkling glow,
With weary feet which to the hearthstone came,
My friend would ask that light be shaded low ;
And then again, to stay mildewing care
From spotting all the colours of the soul
By secret folded thoughts, he would declare
Of Life, and all its purposes unroll.
And when unburthened, with awakened smile
Ask for a rhyme, the moments to beguile.

Hespera ! standing between day and night
We pause, whilst looking at thy gliding feet,
Which come with rose tints of the sunset light,
And noiseless pass, enwrapped in shadows swect.

LILIAN.

ENWRAPT in thought, mild Lilian sate
In an embrasure, where the light
Streamed from on high, and dancing bright
Played in her golden hair, which late

Unbound and from its coils set free,
As happy thoughts imprisoned long
Burst forth in gay tumultuous song,
So frolicked it in liberty ;

Adown her shoulders lithe and small
Tumbling in all its glittering sheen,
As cloth of gold that robes a queen
Low to the ground in folds doth fall ;

And shining like a nimbus round
A very sweet and gentle face,
Whose charm was but the reflex grace
That aye with loving heart is found.

A panelled picture old and quaint
Her mirror gives, where is enshrined
Meekness and gravity combined,
Befitting well a maiden saint.

But Lilian's eyes not in her glass
Are resting, but with quiet smile
Upon her lap intent, the while
Her fingers slight the needle pass ;

Whilst, with an artist's taste and skill,
She blends the silks that ev'ry flower
Speaks to the soul with mystic power,
As though it bloomed by vale or hill.

And many an anxious thought and care,
And many a moment stol'n away,
Had Lilian given day by day
To make this 'broidery rich and rare.

" Gift won is not heart won," she sighed ;
" Yet this may prove the cunning key
Which shall at last unlock for me
The treasure hitherto denied."

She smiled.   " It is so dainty fine,
The wand'ring bees will hither come,
And think they're in their garden home,
Upon thy gown, O sister mine !

" This ophrys, spotted gold and brown,
In mimic semblance may beguile
Their little wings to pause awhile,
Ere they will dare to settle down.

" These flowers of Spring in love I drew—
Pale oxalis with purple veins,
That hiding in the wood remains,
And yellow paigle wet with dew."

A sound as of an opening door,
A shadow on the mirror cast,
And a firm footstep quickly passed
Across the room, across the floor.

A stately form, a form of pride,
A face in Beauty's perfect grain,
That but to look on it again,
Both men and maids would turn aside.

Thus hastily surprised, all mazed
Down thrust were silken skeins confused,
And, archly smiling, half amused,
Lilian her slender arms upraised ;

And, as if that her sole employ,
Slowly and dreamily she weaves
Her fingers through her hair, and leaves
Them resting there as if in joy.

But quick her timid lids again
Droop tremulous ; a sudden chill
Pales brow and cheek, as thro' her thrill
The swift-winged words of cold disdain.

" Said I not well in scorn of late,
That ever false was over sweet ?
That low-voiced tones were ever meet
With cunning and sly craft to mate ?

" When saintly Lilian oft retires
For holy orison and prayer,
This is the sacred work which there
Her chamber's solitude inspires ;

" This the device through which she's dight
With praise of men in foolish rhymes ;
By these arts did she lure betimes
A heart that was mine own by right.

" So sirens, with melodious song,
And shining hair all spread around
(In the old myths), successful found
Such arts to subjugate the strong.

" In careless seeming, but with aim
As one at home in small deceits,
This paper with its fond conceits
Must needs my eye's attention claim,

" As if to make parade, I trow,
Of triumphs, since she's not too fair ;
But then she hath such wondrous hair,
And its achievements I must know ! "

Once, as the bitter accents fell,
Lilian her trembling fingers prest
Slightly her bosom's sacred nest ;
And then, as if the passing bell

Had tolled her young life's years, the flush,
That had but for a moment's space
In crimson dyed her brow and face,
Fled backward with a sudden rush.

She spoke not, for the blood was chilled
In her warm veins, and semblant death
Stayed the pulsations of her breath,
As those words' meaning thro' her thrilled.

But as the sense she was alone
Came back to her, then came again
Quick heart-throbs of a greater pain,
Of wrong for which she must atone.

And hastily she strove to scan

The lines that were before her flung,

These lines o'er which she fondly hung

With the first dawn that day began ;

Lines that with eager smiles she read,

And childlike wonderment of joy,

That in the present no alloy

Can find, no unfaith, and no dread.

But now each word a deeper cloud

Hangs in dark shadow o'er her brow ;

These thoughts in all their onward flow

And tinkling rhymes do untruth shroud.

A little bird which roamed a garden's sphere,
And saw within the fine meshed nets secured,
The pale and ruddy currants close immured,
Hovered with longings all the day anear,

And finds at last an entrance ; but affright
At being captured now its bosom thrills,
That which it so desired seems fraught with ills,
Its one aim now, its sole idea—flight.

Its flutterings vain a friendly eye that sees,
With gentle hand the envious cords removes,
Bares the ripe fruit the speckled songster loves,
And the bright clusters with the poor bird frees.

But now it pauseth not to gaze anew
Where hang the careless berries without let,
More beautiful in freedom : how forget
The peril 'scaped, the prison yet in view ?

And so right joyous, lifting high glad wings,
It seeks its safety in the wood's retreat,
Where, heedless of the coveted escheat,
In loud melodious throbs its freedom sings.

But erst, when captured in a silken net
My Lilian's tresses closely lay confined,
I found to that small prison house assigned
The dearest wishes of my heart had met.

Nor sought I to be free ; but when in grace
My lady would her prisoner restore,
And loosed the cords, I saw, unseen before,
Each golden hair did fetters interlace.

O gold-rayed lily ! for my crest
I take thee from this hour :
My love's pale brow, her radiant crown,
The quiet majesty which dwells
In the deep calm of her pure breast,
To my heart's every thought, to my whole being tells
Of thee, thou stately regal flower !

This reading, with sad 'wildered gaze
Towards her mirror's page she bent ;
The silent mirror backward lent
A vision seen with flushed surprise.

Upon her hands her head drooped low ;
Her lips, with half suppressèd cry,
Broke forth with " Oh, my mother, why
Hast thou then left me ? Thou didst know

" My weakness. I am as a reed
Swaying, and to the breeze inclined ;
Made strong in fellowship, but by th' wind
Prostrated ; standing lone, in need.

" Was she the first loved ? Could it be
That these poor threads of gold could sway
A true heart from its faith away ?
And comes this grief to her through me ? "

Then suddenly she rose. A light
Illumined her like that which gleamed
From Holy Stephen's face, when beamed
His dying brow with radiance bright.

" If it be so, the love that 'bides
True to itself and love, must dare
All sacrifice, and nurse no snare
Which love from love's perfecting hides."

All high resolve is strength ; where late
Each nerve in her slight figure shook
With sense of pain, too great to brook
Withouten lapse a jealous hate,

Now seemed as firmly strung as those
Which, when preparing for the race,
With brightened eye and purposed face,
The young athlete's strong limbs disclose :

As void of passion or quick haste
With an untrembling hand and slow,
Severed glide silently below
The glittering locks, in cruel waste ;

And Lilian standeth there alone,
As the dark shadows steal along,
Shorn of her glory—theme of song
That oft had woke th' uncertain tone

Of youth's poetic strain ; more dear
The well-remembered fond caress,
When a loved mother's hand did press
The clustering curls and forehead clear.

Thrice did the bell with shrill resound,
In louder tones its summons peal,
To gather for the evening meal ;
And thrice the echoes died around.

And in the shadows there alone
She stood so still, her bosom's swell
Scarce stirred her white robe's folds, which fell
In simple lines, like sculptured stone.

But starting suddenly, she clasps
Her hands, as one bounds up the stair,
Humming a careless, merry air,
And quick the chamber door unhasps.

And Mabel's voice is heard again,
And, somewhat like the bittersweet,
Where poisons and where beauty meet,
A sportive jest now points the strain.

" Has not the gold-rayed lily yet
Its crown arranged ? We wait below
All anxious, curious to know
The cause which doth its coming let.

" And Herbert too is there, and wears
In sort sublime his chains. They seem
To gall him somewhat, so I deem
From the grave knitted brow he bears."

One moment more, and Lilian flung
Herself athwart her sister's breast,
And the soul's feelings, unreprest,
Burst from her lips as there she clung.

C

" Give me thy heart.   I did not know
Until this hour where lay offence ;
But it was late revealed, and hence
I ask thy love—with fearless brow.

" If I am weeping, be content ;
It is not for my beauty lost—
It is not that I count the cost
But all too late, and now repent.

" For Herbert thou art fittest bride.
How will his pencil joy to trace
For ever in thy form and face
A subject for his art and pride ! "

Tumultuous quick sense of shame,
Prelude to justice and to right,
Shrinketh before the sudden light,
Not strong to meet the inner blame.

So Mabel quick those arms unwound,
And fled with sobbing.   Well she knew
His place was there, in whose heart true
Unswerving loyalty was found.

And Herbert kneels at Lilian's feet,
And murmurs, " Though thy golden hair
Was precious in my sight, more fair
Thou seemest now.   O love ! O sweet !

" Ungentle hands my lily flower
Have harshly bruised ; but by God's will,
'Neath careful tending, it shall still
Bloom in a storm-sequestered bower."

THE VOICES THREE.

THE weaving it stays not by night or day,
The colours dazzle with lurid light,
With shining trails and flashes bright,
But crossed with shadows every way;
And a lady of beauty, with smile of doom,
Sits at the wheel, or stands by the loom,
    And ever singeth she this song—
    " I spin deftly, I weave strong."

The threads have been spun by that lady weird–
Threads of gold and of fibres fine,
Fit and meet for the subtle twine
Of a woof whose weaving for men's souls spiered

And with careful eye the lady drew
Closely the threads as the warp she threw,
　　And this the burden of her song—
　　" I spin deftly, I weave strong."

A knight there lay where the moonbeams fell,
In couchèd softness and liddèd sleep ;
And all enwound in the mystic keep
Of the fine-spun threads of unholy spell ;
For aye as the thread had lengthened out,
The lady had coiled him with loops about,
　　And grimly smiling sung her song—
　　" I spin deftly, I weave strong."

There came a noise of tramping steeds,
The rouse of a martial strain,
A trumpet blew shrilly again and again,
Calling a summons to hero's deeds.

The lady she looked where the warrior lay ;
And his limbs they stirred.   It passed away,
> And she laughed in scorn, and sung her
> song—
> " I spin deftly, I weave strong."

Through the thick tapestries there came
Floating chant of the hymnal praise,
Old chapelries were wont to raise
At eve to Holy Mary's name.
" Alma Redemptoris mater ;" and high
Rung one clear voice, as seeming nigh.
> The lady she frownèd in her song—
> " I spin deftly, I weave strong."

As the chorus rose, as the chorus fell,
The knight his heavy lids ope'd wide,
Slightly moaned, and turned on his side ;
But still she wove her magic spell.

"Peccatorum miserere," in accents fair,
Tremblingly died in the shadowy air.
        The lady laughed again in her song—
        "I spin deftly, I weave strong."

The night was gloomy, the night was still,
And thro' the silence there came a cry
As of a woman and child close by,
And their tender wailing the room did fill.
Of sobbing and kisses there came a sound,
And the snap of a thread at a sudden bound.
        But the lady paused not in her song—
        "I spin deftly, I weave strong."

The knight again hath sunk to his sleep,
The lady rises from woof and web :
"A time for flow, a time for ebb ;
The voices three have spoken deep.

There cometh none other to mar my sway,

When those voices three have died away.

I stay my warp, I stay my song,

Spinning deftly, weaving strong."

MYRA.

" Mourir pour la patrie
C'est le mort le plus beau, le plus digne d'envie."

" DEAR child, upon this ancient tome
Mine eye and brain have pondered long,
And still the meaning hath not come,
Though busy fancies thickly throng.

" So, Myra, whilst I rest awhile,
Read me some old romantic lay,
Such as may troublous thoughts beguile,
Such as may passion's dreams assway."

And Myra rose in slender grace,
And reached a once-lov'd volume down,

And bending low her glowing face
(Which trembled with a little frown,

To see that dust had gathered there),
She read, in mellow tones and clear,
Of warrior knight and lady fair,
And truth, to constant hearts so dear.

And as her accents rose and fell,
With passion or with pathos sweet,
Within the room, as by a spell,
The poet's phantoms straight did meet,

And held me in a mystic chain ;
Nor knew I when, but only knew,
And knew it with a sense of pain,
The voice was hushed, and silence grew.

But fixed was Myra's steadfast look
On the still open page, and where

There lay upon the printed book
A crispèd lock of chestnut hair.

    *   *   *   *   *

" I heard the throstles yester eve,
Where the tall elm trees shadows long ᾿
Fling on the grass, as loth to leave ;
We will go listen to their song."

And Myra nothing said, but rose
And softly linked her arm in mine,
And thus we passed the garden rows,
Where showed her care and culture fine ;

Nor paused until we reached the gate,
Round which the woodbine frolics free,
, Where the elm shadows ling'ring wait,   ,
And there upon a fallen tree

We sat, and listened to the song,
Through which the refrain ever swept,

" Life it is short, but love is long,'
And then I knew that Myra wept.

I stooped to kiss her drooping head,
Whilst softly fast the tear-drops fell.
" Did he not well, dear child ?" I said ;
And Myra answered, " He did well."

POPPIES.

I.

POPPIES ! the bright red poppies here again,
With smell of new-mown hay !
Poppies ! that like all loved things bring some
     pain
That lingers near them alway—yes, alway.
Poppies that once ('tis many years ago)
Set my heart all aflame with ruddy light,
As they were nestling in a gown of white.

II.

A bunch of poppies anywhere and how
Is still a glorious sight ;
Yet I would travel on by day and night,

If only once to see the fields where grew

Those poppies that beneath cathedral shade

One afternoon ('tis many years ago)

Gleamed on me as the swelling organ played,

Filling the hollow dome with echoes deep and
      low,

Whilst men and boys in full-toned quire did
      raise

Sweet Mary's loving song of grateful praise.

A richer mellowed treble on my ear

Than boys can give, had fallen with a thrill ;

A tender tremor filling all space near

With its pathetic sentience of God's will ;

And I looked up, and saw a clear pale face,

Set round in crisping waves of nut-brown hair,

Shine midst the dark carved oak in radiant
      grace

Like to some holy thing, it was so fair.

And as of handmaid's lowliness they sang,

Tears in her eyes of purple gray I saw ;

Tears such as Gabriel might have witnessed
    hang,

On lids that drooped in meekness to God's law.

Gazing, my thoughts as in a dream

Were borne away from earth to spirits blest,

When suddenly I saw the gleam

Of poppies lying on her breast ;

And, rich in life, a warming glow

They upward cast and 'round on that pale face
    and garb of snow.

III.

O poppies ! ye awoke me to a smile

Of earth and earth joys, when

Was lost straightway the heavenly strain awhile ;

And the awaking then,

Has thrown my whole life backward to a dream

In shadow land, whilst walking to and fro,

Holding a guiding lantern, with the gleam
Of poppies resting amid folds of snow.

IV.

I heard nor text nor preacher.   She
Who sat there list'ning, rapt and lost,
Both text and preacher was to me ;
And through the long years, tempest tost,
No sweeter teaching yet to me hath come,
Than there I learnt beneath cathedral dome.

V.

There came a rustle and a pause,
The preacher's voice was still, and then
The murmured " Peace of God "—the cause,
So little understood of men.
Bowed were all heads the blessed gift to meet
And poppies' petals fluttered to my feet.

VI.

Her skirts they brushed me as she passed along

From out the porch, the marble steps then down ;

One hand was linked within an arm right strong,

The other slightly raised her snow-white gown.

A smile was dawning o'er her stainless cheek,

As he who held her arm within his own,

Bade her in loving jest her poppies seek,

From whence the crumpled petals thin had
  flown,

And the bare calices, bereft,

Upon her bosom sadly drooping left.

VII.

And she was gone! the horses' heels

Threw on my brow the splashing soil.

And she was gone! the carriage wheels

Sped swiftly through the thick turmoil,

D

To bear her back to country life,

To poppy-fields and waving grass ;

Whilst I, who held a heart with love's thoughts
     rife,

With slowly dragging feet did homeway pass.

VIII.

Upon my psalter's page I laid

The wayward petals, one by one,

Which, from their stalklets having strayed,

I gathered from the pavement stone.

I saw their colour day by day,

As by remorseful sorrow stained,

Not fade, but sadly change away

Till only funeral tints remained.

IX.

Still, when the bell for evensong

Fell on my anxious list'ning ear,

I threaded through the busy throng,

And sought the holy temple near.

And day by day I felt my heart

Beat with a feeling ever new ;

And day by day with sudden start

Of quickened pulses, when I knew

(Although I dared not look around)

That in that oak carved shadowy stall,

Of rustling robes there came a sound.

O God ! the tears that there did fall

In secret, on that holy floor,

Were not for youthful sins, but that *she* came

    no more.

X.

I saw her never more—no more,

And that is many years ago,

And in the world, from shore to shore,

I have still wandered to and fro.

The world is but a speck in space,

To me it seemeth wondrous large,

Since, one day looking on a face,

I knew it took my life in charge;

And sought it fervently, as some seek gold,

And sought it vainly, till the years grew old.

XI.

To-day I lie amongst the uncut grass,

With the blithe poppies waving o'er my brow;

And there I dream and dream, and sweetly pass

Away from all the present and the now:

And I again am 'neath cathedral dome,

And I again behold a presence come,

And I again do hear sweet tones rehearse,

" My soul doth magnify the Lord," in touching

    solemn verse.

XII.

But it is yet day, tho' the night be near,
And I wake up to life and work again ;
Nor will the poppies grieve that I shall bear
An armful with me homewards.   An old strain
Will through the silent chamber steal,
And rain down harmonies on my lone meal ;
Whilst o'er the well-filled vase will droop,
And to the white-clothed board will stoop,
The ruddy blossoms, bringing near
A contrast that so long ago,
Impanelled in my heart most clear,
Was pictured on a robe of snow.
And gazing in them I shall therein see
Those thoughtful eyes of deepest violet gray,
In petals purple based which will not flee
Nor close, till wearily they drop away,
Falling upon the damask one by one,
As some fell once upon cathedral stone.

XIII.

So pass the days in works which make some
    glad,
So pass the nights in thoughts which are not
    sad ;
Betwixt the heavens and earth, in loving tending,
The messengers, the angels, still are wending.

XIV.

Yet, when my earth's last evensong is sung,
And "Nunc dimittis " is my call to rest,
Friends! when the passing bell its knell hath
    rung,
Lay ye a bunch of poppies on my breast :
For that I do believe most solemnly,
My summons hence will most assured be
In summer-tide, when July's glowing time
Is bathing all the earth in golden prime.

And, friends ! in some green spot where grasses
    wave,

There (unencased) just scoop a little grave,

And lay me down where laughing poppies grow ;

Of which the children, running to and fro,

Will fill their laps, whilst singing joyful rhymes ;

And whither there may come by chance some-
    times

A maiden such as she, who'll bare her hand

To pluck them, whilst her pausing feet will
    stand

Upon that peaceful sod—one whose heart's
    shrine,

As hers, is templed by a love divine.

ELFIE'S DOLL.

ONE morning as I walked along, on many a
    tortuous thought intent,
Elfie, a little maiden child with large gray eyes
    of solemn bent,
I overtook, as to and fro she moved with grave
    and quiet pace,
And all the cares of motherhood upon her
    little matron face.

" Elfie, do let me see your doll," I asked ; but
    she relaxed no whit
Her tightly clasping arms, but pursed her rosy
    lips a tiny bit,

And looked at me with doubting, as she
    answered, very firm and slow,
" What can *you* want to see her for ?—indeed, I
    should much like to know."

Now, Elfie's doll had had some wear, for then
    there was not left a trace
Of any bloom on cheek, or lip, in her poor
    mealy washed out face ;
And Elfie's doll had lost an eye, its head was
    dented in, and bare ;
And, I suspect, of legs and arms it did not boast
    the usual share.

" Now, Elfie," said I, coaxingly, "will you not
    kindly give it me ? "
The little maiden frowned severe, and hugged it
    still more fervently.

"Give it to me, my Elfie dear ; will you not truly
    love me so ? "
But Elfie only frowned the more, and very
    sternly answered, " No."

" Nay, but instead I'll bring to you one other
    showing much more fair,
With bright blue eyes, and rosy cheeks,
And long and glossy golden hair ;
With waxen arms and feet ;—indeed, the prettiest
    creature that is sold,
If you to me will give that doll, so very ugly,
    worn, and old."

Then Elfie with her large gray eyes looked up
    at once into my face,
And she stopped her hushing "bye-bye," and
    she stayed her solemn matron pace ;

And with a tighter clasping still, in ringing
    words distinct and slow,
With measured utterance she spoke, as her
    indignant thought did grow.

" Go, then, and buy yourself that doll, so much
    more pretty and more fair,
With bright blue eyes, and rosy cheeks, and
    long and glossy golden hair ;
And I will have my own doll—yes, my own doll
    I will keep alway ;
I will not have your new doll, no, for all the
    words that you may say."

And Elfie is a woman now, her eyes are large
    and clear and gray ;
But when I ask her of her doll, she laughs with
    scorn, and turns away—

She says she has forgotten quite, and it must be
a great mistake,
So hideous an object ne'er one thought from her
could scarcely take.

But Elfie 'tis who erreth—who, alas! can now
in no wise see,
What mystery of love lay shrouded in the
mem'ry she doth flee;
Nor knows she when her grand and clear gray
eyes look proudly in my face,
I miss with sighs the beauty of her childhood's
sweet and loyal grace.

QUEEN VASHTI.

THE wine is flashing high
  Where King Ahasuerus holds his feast ;
  There is no stint or measure in the cup,
  With precious metals worked, which joys the
    eye.
  To-day restraining rules are all releast ;
  " Fill up the quick-drained goblet, fill it up."

On beds of gold reclined
  The king with all his princes.   On the walls
  Rich many-coloured hangings draped around,
  Fine purple fillets to the pillars bind
  On silver rings.   Each heavy fold down falls
  On porphyry and jasper marbled ground.

Shall not Queen Vashti come ?

This is the seventh day of deep carouse,

The king's proud heart is burning hot within ;

He looks upon his royal state and home.

What is there more his nobles to arouse,

To sense of all his majesty therein ?

" Will the Queen Vashti come ? "

Said one to other with full beakers raised ;

Whispered, with eyes lit up with wanton fire,

Across the laughter-sparkling beads of foam ;

" Shall we look on the beauties so much

     praised ? "

Let Vashti come, was each lewd heart's desire.

" Bid our Queen Vashti here,

To show her hidden fairness us among,

That we may gaze, and thereof take our fill.

Then shall ye say she is without compeer

'Mongst womankind who have been sung in
    song ;
And she too waiteth on my kingly will."

" Will not Queen Vashti come ? "
    She sitteth with her women, as the moon
    Among the stars in majesty and grace,
    In the veiled precincts of her regal home,
    Which guards with jealous eye the golden noon
    From looking on the glories of her face.

Queen Vashti veils her brow.
    " What saith the king thy lord, my lord the
        king ?
    Hath he not drunken deep for seven days ?
    The strong wine doth his goblet overflow ;
    He understandeth not what unclean thing
    This mandate on his queen and handmaid lays.

" What message bring'st me now ?

   It seemeth me a mockery and jest!

   Great Ahasuerus has too much forgot.

   Am I a dancing girl with bold bare brow,

   To curve myself and smile to please a guest ?

   To the king's feast Queen Vashti goeth not.

" Vashti am I, the queen!

   A consort fitted for so great a king,

   Who chooseth not as shepherds choose theii

      mates ;

   The honour of my lord the king is seen

   To suffer, if his handmaid in this thing

   The dignity of queenliness abates.

" As Vashti, she hath more,

   The garment of her womanhood to bear,

   That on her cheek ne'er riseth clouding shame

   When she doth stand her lord the king before ;

That is her own possession, which to wear

Unsullied, honoureth the king's great name.

" Say to my lord the king,

His handmaid's life, her royal state, her crown,

Were his to grant, are his to take away ;

That these she to his feet will humbly bring :

Yet of herself, when these she layeth down,

Discrowned or crowned, Vashti is queen

alway."

E

THE POET'S WIFE.

My head is weary with a sense of loss,
Although the summer-tide is all aglow ;
Whate'er I look upon seems turned to dross,
With thoughts that stifle, and with thoughts that
    grow.

I knew it was my beauty woke his theme,
Mine eyes that made his verse with passion flow,
And I was proud and happy.   Did I deem
That he would mount, whilst I was left below ?

The years have made him famous, and the years
Have weighed upon me with exceeding weight ;
Betwixt us two, there day by day appears
A deeper valley, and a steeper height.

Did I not see the looks of cold surprise,
When on his arm amid the courtly hall?
The questioning glances and uplifted eyes,
As though they whispered, " Does her face recall

Aught that could e'er those glowing lines inspire
Which on a sudden made the world to pause
And ask with rapture, 'Whence caught he this
    fire?'
Who is the maid, and where, that is the cause?"

And so I go no more to clog his joy
With the sad thought I am no fitting mate
For his ripe years; he was but yet a boy
When for my " starry eyes " he tempted fate.

All day I sit alone, and on my knees
His poems lie open, and I strive in vain
To lift my soul to his; my weak brain sees
Words, words, and only words, and words again.

But yet I will not tell him I have grief,

For he would seek in some way to atone ;

I would not see, for my poor heart's relief,

My eagle moping by the ingle stone.

THE FOUNDERING OF THE "CYPRIAN." *

"O HO, merrily ho!

We are riding to port, and I see the line

Of the coast and the harbour. There is a glow

That tells thro' the mist that the moon will shine,

To light us home,

O'er the waves and foam,

To the hearts and hearths

That are warm and bright;

God give us joy of our meeting to-night!"

A smile came over the master's face,

As the good ship *Cyprian* danced along;

He was sure of the grounding and every trace,

And his heart leaped up in a merry song,

* The *Cyprian* foundered off Wales in the autumn of 1881. The master, John Strachan, gave his own and last life-belt to a stowaway, and was drowned.

"Ha! ha! for the mariner coming ashore,
For of all his long watches as many more
Are the kisses in store."
The master stopped in his low-voiced song.
"Take your soundings, the fog is coming along!
The shores of our land are treacherous oft;
Its children, homeward bound,
Too often have met with a rough embrace,
Too often a grave have found,
When they thought that a few hours, more or less,
Would find them clasped in their mothers' arms.
Look out to the windward!"
What saith the lead,
That there drifts a gloom o'er the master's face,
Where late the dream of a fond caress
Had left the light of its passing trace,

But now is shadowed by growing dread ?

" We are foundering, mate! the rocks are ahead !

Now God give us help, and Christ send grace,

For we have sailed straight for our burial-place!

I thank Thee, Father, that on this day

Nor woman, nor child, doth with me stay !

Steady and calm ! let down the boat,

And save ye, my men, and one by one,

And without a tremor now get ye afloat,

And God guide ye safe to the unkind shore.

I will bide me here, and see that none

Be left to perish, and I, alone,

Will trust to the waves that have ofttimes bore

Me safe on their bosom. This life-belt good

Will aid me to brave the darkling flood."

Down thro' the darkness and the gloom

Dropped the boat on the sullen sea,
And one by one, and silently,
The men they wrung the master's hand,
As they passed before where he did stand,
And gave to each a belt for need
If the boat should swamp, and to each " God
    speed."

The master stood on the deck alone,
His life-belt in his hand ;
His burthened heart gave forth a groan
For the safety of his band,
And he looked around with a noble joy
That he was but one, and they were gone.
And then he thought of his wife and boy
In their cottage home alone,
And his broad breast heaved as he raised his arms

To plunge in the hissing wave.

His heart it beat with no vague alarms,

For the master was good and brave.

But his arm was seized with convulsive grip,

And a gasping voice in his ear outshrieked,

"Am I to go down with your rotten ship?

Am I to be left to be murdered and wrecked,

Whilst the others go safe to land?"

And a ghastly wretch, in frantic fear,

Clutched at the master with nerveless hand.

"Who art *thou*, man? whence, why art thou here?

Thou art not one of my faithful crew,

Who sailed with me o'er the tropic seas;

I counted them all to the boat—they were few—

I could not misdoubt, for I saw them and know

That nine was their number who went below.

" Nor art thou one of the voyagers three ;

They were my first care, my mind to ease.

I know thee now—yes, thou art he

The stowaway, who basely found

A hiding-place the bales among ;

And when our ship was under sail

Crept forth, and raised our good mate's ire,

Who swore such cumbrance of the ground

Should to the fishes straight be flung.

Stand up, man ! If I did now fail

In doing that which I judged right,

Before I met this purging fire,

There might be some excusing plea

In that poor babe and mother frail,

Who by the morn for such as thee

Will widow and will orphan be.

"Take now this belt, and for I know
Thou wilt not dare to plunge below,
And that full oft I've made the vow
That never would I leave my prow
In any peril, any woe,
That oft befalls those sons of men,
Who down to the deep in ships do go
And see God's wonders clearly then.
Here I remain : but stand aside —
Nor say I this in foolish pride
To bid thee go apart ;
But that, in face of coming ill,
It best befitteth human heart
To commune, and be still.
Yet heed these words : if thou through grace
Dost reach the shore alive,

" Keep thou a cleaner breast—
No man defraud, but henceforth strive
To owe to no one aught,
Save that which with all good is fraught ;
If not, God give thee rest."

The master folded his hands in prayer,
And his head bowed on his breast :
" God ! Thou art holy, and just, and good ;
And for Thy guiding care
Until this hour, Thy name be blest ! "

THE TRYSTING TREE.

THREE EPOCHS.

SOFT is the wind that is stirring the grass
Where is sleeping the pale anemone ;
I heed not the moments which sweetly pass.
Pink and white blossoms are clust'ring the tree.

    *   *   *   *   *

Bright is the sun that is gliding each bough,
Bright are the smiles that are greeting me,
Bright is the golden hair shading a brow,
Ruddy red apples hang thick on the tree.

    *   *   *   *   *

I have waited here till the shadows come,
I have waited long whilst the hours flee,
I am waiting still in the mist and the gloom.
One by one fall the dead leaves from the tree.

THE SUDDEN CLOUD.

As erst I looked upon my dear love's brow,
Where shone the summer of a sweet content,
Amazed I saw a sudden shadow grow,
And all the sunlight in a moment shent.

Taking her hand, " Nay, sweet, whence comes this
    cloud
Unheralded that thus doth bring alloy ? "
Her tear - gemmed eyes this rising thought
    avowed—
" Grief treadeth still upon the heels of joy."

TO KALLIOPE.

NAY, frown not, sweet Athenian maid,
At this my gift of asphodels.
Believe me, that these graceful bells
Were gathered in no gloomy shade ;
For had I trod that fated plain
Where memory ceases, thee again
I had not sought, forgotten evermore the pleasure
    and the pain.

DORA; OR, LAST WORDS.

" DRAW back the curtain, let me see the sky :
There are so many shadows in the room
Which come and go, for ever passing by,
Hiding from me the light in misty gloom.
Dear wife, come nearer to me, sit beside,
And raise my head that I may look again
Upon the sunset in its crimson pride.
Nay, it is yet too much, too great a strain ;
Let fall, and listen as I speak awhile
Of that which is the burden of my heart.
The grateful thoughts I bear thee make a pile
Too heavy for my feeble words t' impart.
Ah ! thou wert ever diligent and kind
To meet my crudest wishes.   In the years

That follow after this drear time, thou'lt find

This knowledge will make transient all sad tears.

I fear to thee I have been sorry mate—

A selfish bookworm, reading midnight hours,

And oft till morning at the eastern gate

Came gliding in to waken up the flowers.

But it is all now past. If there was aught

That ever vexed thee in my silent mood,

Thou knowest yet that I have ever sought

To reverence in thee the wise and good.

The future will be easy for thee, dear;

That was my earliest, my chiefest care,

So thou might'st never feel the anxious fear

That goes where needs do doubtful fortunes
     dare.

No, there is nothing more, and I am weak :

Dear wife, thy hand is heavy on my brow.

I will now sleep. But, Agnes, if I speak

In all my wandering dreams, belike I may,

F

Thou wilt not heed.   Now rest thee, rest thee,
     drear
Thy watch has been—thy watch by night and day
Most long, most weary ! rest thee, rest thee, dear.
In a sick room, where Death is hovering near,
How many angel feet do walk unseen !
How many angel whisperings you hear
The watches of the deep-browed night between,
When skilled Love, not the hired watcher, tends
And the wife Agnes had the dext'rous hand
Whose gentleness expert its tendance lends
In unfelt, unknown touches ; no command
T'obey, because each need was seen before
The feeble lips the halting phrase could frame.
How slowly drag the minutes thro' each hour,
After the dial a fresh day doth name !
With what relief is seen the first pale streak
That pierces the closed blinds, and brings the
     chill

Which heralds in the dawn, and shows the cheek,

Than yesterday more wan and haggard still !

And Agnes sat beside, but yet not close,

In deference to the dying husband's mind,   '

Which cared not for caresses : one of those

Whose ways are reticent and cold, but kind.

And thus *her* manner by communion grew

Repressive of emotional warm glow :

Gracious to all, and friendly to the few

Who, like her husband, scholar tastes did show.

She sits beside him, in her features blend

Some pride along with sadness ; though no tears

Swell the full lids, the eyes cease not to bend

Ward unremitting, lest some change appears.

And he is sleeping—that deep sleep which oft

Slopes into, or precursor is of death.

Across his face there stole expression soft ;

His lips were moving with a quickened breath ;

His opened eyes shone with a stranger light ;
And with convulsive force his arms stretched forth
Towards, as if to clasp her.　Quick as light
She sank down closer to him, as most loth
To lose *last precious words.*　He gave a sigh,
And looked at her with strained and wandering
　　　gaze,
With a half-timid yet dilated eye,
As he were seeking something through a haze ;
And then the broken words came trembling
　　　through
In accents strange and foreign to her ear,
With fond impassioned tenderness which grew
To full heart-chords of throbbing tones and clear.
"Dora! my own dear Dora! sweet one! place
Thy hand in mine, my own love! on my brow
Drop thy cool kisses!　Do not hide thy face,
But look at me, my sweet, for well I know
Thou hast not lost one atom of thy grace.

Yet, love, thou must be weary : it is long
Since thy dear head hath lain it down to sleep.
I now am happy, Dora. Yesterday
I could not speak thy name, my Dora—no,
Nor yesterday nor many days : there lay
A spell upon me, why I do not know,
Because I see thee, and thou art not dead,
But yet I *dared* not *Dora* say aloud ;
I whispered it sometimes with hushing breath,
Lest other one should hear. Ah, what a crowd
There came to see us wedded ! I was sad ;
Thou didst not wear thy usual face that day.
But it is long ago, and I am glad
That time is past, for ever gone away.
Thy little hand is trembling ! Go and sleep
Awhile, my Dora darling ! I will call
If I shall need thee. Dear love, do not weep ;
Ah, do not so ! I am not sad at all :
I seem as I had travelled long and far,

And borne a heavy burthen all the way.

At nights there never came one shimmering star ;

The days were very cloudy, dull alway.

I worked and worked, and studied hard and late

To get me from myself, and now they say

My brain hath been o'ercharged.   No; it was hate

Of thy strange look upon our marriage day :

For, ever after, ever until now,

I thought it was not Dora I had wed.

This foolish thought dug furrows on my brow ;

This foolish thought gnawed so till my heart bled :

And now I am a worn and dying man,

And all because of that same foolish thought

Which blurred me so, that now I cannot see

Thy features, my own Dora, as I ought—

Not even now, this moment, O my sweet !

When I look fully at thee as just now.

Be thou not angry, darling ! thy dear feet

Need not to beat the floor : but kiss my brow

Again—again, to drive that face away!

Nay, I will close my eyes, or I shall dream ;

My brain is 'wildered.   Art thou Dora ? say,

Oh, say thou'rt Dora !   Hide that hard lamp's

  gleam

That gives another face !   Oh, let me die,

With my own Dora I have loved so long

Kissing my trembling lips.   Say, ' It *is I*,

Thy Dora.'   Ah, the name is like a song

Heard once in childhood and forgot, yet when

'Tis heard again, it is a sounding joy

The years between have never known till then.

Dora !   *my* Dora !   kiss me on my mouth !

It is a foolish thought, yet ere I die,

In those soft tones thou caught'st in the sweet

  south,

Say once—for I am ill—' *Thy* Dora.'   I——"

A troubled tremor for a moment swept

Across the face of her who knelt beside ;

Then o'er her cheek a tender flushing crept,

Lower and lower bent her head of pride.

She kissed him on the mouth—again—again,

And whispered, " I am Dora ; it is I,

Thy love, thy Dora, by thy bed of pain

Watching alway—thy darling Dora, I."

Around her neck his arms essayed to meet ;

A bright smile flickered o'er him.   " Then I die

Most happy.   O my Dora ! bless thee, sweet !

A foolish thought—but Dora could not lie."

And thus, while hot tears rained upon his brow,

His life with kisses gently passed away,

Leaving behind the halo and the glow

Of blissful sweet contentment where he lay ;

Not paler than that tear-stained marble face

Which looked upon him with such pity deep

As guardian angels show, whose helpful grace

Has worked in vain.   A thousand mem'ries

    sweep

Tumultuous, as she strove to bridge the gap

Of that which was, with that which might have

      been.

Some knowledge, if it comes full late, mayhap

If earlier by no better light is seen.

" At last I know the travail of thy soul ;

At last thy lips have quivered to my touch ;

At last, when thou wast drawing to Life's goal—

At last I see thou could'st love overmuch !

This other one, *this Dora*, who is *she*

That thou didst shroud within thy heart so

      long,

Whilst the remembrance sucked thy life from

      thee,

Making thy breast a prison barred iron strong ?

Thy place was here, thou Dora. What wert thou

To me, that I should lie for thee ? My will

Goes strong to hate thee, but that even now

His dying kiss upon my lips doth thrill,

When he believed me Dora.   Yet he said

His Dora could not lie ; and *I* must sear

My soul with lies to soothe his dying head,

And lull him to his rest.   Ah, husband dear,

My lie was not like Yseult's, when it slew

The sinful but true lover.   Thou poor heart !

They who have never loved, and never knew

Love's loss however lost, have here no part ;

But I have loved thee, husband, thro' the years,

And know the heavy load that thou hast borne.

Who is this Dora, that will give no tears

To wash his brow whose life she made forlorn ?

I know her not, if she were false or true,

Or what her likeness ; hidden tress of hair

As secret treasure hoard ne'er gave its hue,

By careless chance revealed, to say 'twas fair ;

Nor absent thoughts on margin of a book

E'er traced the name of *Dora ;*—yet how meet !

When written down it hath a pretty look,

As for a lover's ear its sound is sweet.

Alas! *my* hand weighed heavy on his brow,

Until as Dora's it was angel light.

Will he be angered if he know it now?

Or shall I still be Dora in his sight?

In the fair glory of Love's perfect day,

Shall there be any longer *two?*   Ah no!

The unloved one is blotted out for aye,

And Dora in his Agnes he will know."

OUR ELSIE.

YES, we always were proud of our Elsie—ay,
    somewhat too proud, I fear,
The ring of her laugh it was ever so joyous, so
    pleasant to hear ;
And her eyes were so bright, and her cheeks were
    so downy and fair,
And a gleam of gold ran through the waves of
    her thick chestnut hair !

Our Elsie still comely as aye ! Yes, wife, I know
    it full well ;
And I need not to speak with the tone of a
    funeral bell,
And you cannot make out why so sullen and
    stern I appear,
Whenever her wedding-day cometh, the joyfullest
    day of the year.

It is that my thoughts they go back to that
    night ten years since at this hour,
When the favours were strewn all about—little
    bows with a tuft of some flow'r :
You, wife, and the girls were as proud and as
    happy as happy could be ;
And our Elsie the brightest of all, with the smiles
    aye so pleasant to see !

And I sat and looked on from my chair by the
    fire, and was glad
Our Elsie had met with a husband with solid
    good gifts as Ned had ;
But yet through my gladness came stealing, un-
    bidden, a shade of regret
For the lad whom I loved as my own son, the
    lad whom I could not forget.

Eh—there was never a lad who could handle the
  plough with more skill,
Or would work late and early as he, with body,
  with soul, and with will ;
There was never a lad more God-fearing : well
  looking was he,
And I aye thought if he lov'd our Elsie, and she
  him, what better could be.

And then just to think, of his being so fond of
  the gold,
He must leave the old place, with the sheep and
  the lambs in the fold—
And the corn he had sown too, just showing so
  green on the ground :
It had broken *my* heart to have gone ere the
  harvest came round.

But he went, and ne'er spoke of our Elsie ; and
 Elsie said nought,
Although she did seem a bit downcast a day or
 two after, I thought.
But I soon heard her singing again, and there-
 fore I surely must know
There was no love between them but yet, I won-
 dered that it could be so.

And every one loveth our Elsie, ay, every one
 speaks of her well ;
Her laugh is so pleasant to hear, and her voice is
 as clear as a bell.
There are some girls whose hearts are as true—
 ah, as true as the gold, and as sweet ;
Yet the men never wait at their bidding, nor lay
 down their lives at their feet.

And so, while ye talked of the morrow, the
    dresses, and gewgaws, and more,
I sat in my chair by the fire, when suddenly in
    at the door
Quick cometh the dear lad I thought of—our
    Harry from over the sea,
Sunburnt and handsome as ever, with eyes over-
    flowing with glee.

Forthwith there were hearty embraces, and many
    a clamour and shout,
" You're just in time, Harry!"   "In time! why,
    pray, what is all this about ? "
And you, wife, you looked in his face, as you
    kissed him, with something of scorn
Saying, laughing, " About ? what about ?   Why
    our Elsie will marry i' the morn."

But I marked, 'mid the merry shrill welcomes
   which rang to the roof,
That our Elsie was not 'mong the greeters, but
   silently standing aloof;
And I marked, when I clutched it with ardour,
   and fervently grasped his broad hand,
That it shook like an aspen—God help me! I
   wonder the poor boy could stand.

The hearts that are joyous, too often are blinded;
   they see not at all
Of the sorrow that standeth beside; and clearly
   I still can recall,
How none saw the pallor that stole through the
   breadth of his bonny brown cheek,
As they called, " Just in time!" But our Elsie,
   our Elsie, she—she—did not speak.

G

But Harry was made of good stuff, wife, that
  night—yes, that night made it plain ;
And although you don't like me to say it, I say
  it, and say it again,
That he was too good for our Elsie, though her
  cheek was so downy and fair,
And though her smiles always were flashing
  from under her waved chestnut hair.

Then he gave a long glance once around, and
  he said, with a somewhat sad smile,
"Nay, I must be gone ere the morrow, and
  travelling many a mile
Ere the joy-bells ring merrily forth ; but although
  I stay not as a guest,
I am glad that I came *just in time*, my bride-gift
  to place with the rest ! "

Then he drew from his bosom a necklet, with
    rubies and pearls all beset,
With curious devices in gold work. " 'Tis Indian.
    I did not forget
That once when the yule log was burning, our
    hearts their dear wishes unbound,
And Elsie she wished for a necklet, with rubies
    and pearls set around."

And straight he went up to our Elsie, who was
    silently standing aloof,
And, though he spoke low, I'll be sworn that he
    uttered no tone of reproof.
I just heard but so much : " Dear Elsie, be happy
    —be happy ! From me
No word that shall trouble thy future shall e'er
    come. There—there—let it be.

" As brother to sister, to thee do I offer these
        jewels, and pray
That as bride and as wife thou wilt wear them in
        sisterly calmness alway.
Farewell ! I can tarry no longer.   Shall I come
        back some day ?   Yes, some day
We   shall   all—we   shall   all—meet   again—
        where——"   He faltered, and hastened
        away.

Now, wife, do not look so afeared, when I tell
        thee my heart felt as cold
As though it was chilled into ice, and its beatings
        for ever outtold,
When one look I gave to our Elsie, who silent
        apart still did stand,
With a flush on her cheek, but a smile—yes, a
        smile at the gems in her hand.

Dearest wife, just for once ask poor Elsie to-
morrow to lay them aside—
Just for once, then perhaps I shall less feel this
dull heavy pain at my side—
For ever I think I behold, as I look on those
rubies and pearls,
Large blood-drops and tears trickling down,
though the eyes laugh from under the
curls.

But whilst all were praising the baubles, and
wond'ring and crying aloud,
Of their beauty and worth, and some added,
" How odd Harry was, and how proud ! "
I stole unobserved from the room, and I quietly
followed him out,
For I said to myself I knew well that the lad
would be somewhere about.

And I went where I thought to be sure I should
　　find him, but he was not there,
Though the foal had been just like his own child,
　　and often you'd heard me declare,
That one of the first of his wishes, if ever the
　　lad should come home,
Would be just to know of the brown foal, and
　　what of its promise had come.

But as I came round through the gate by the
　　orchard, right close to the seat,
Which Harry's own hand had upbuilded so
　　cleverly, dainty, and neat,
With branches all close interwoven and carefully
　　canopied round,
With logs quaintly carved just for footstools
　　placed firmly and sunk in the ground ;—

I heard a loud crying of anguish, and there came
    thro' the heavy night air
The wail of a strong man in travail—in travail
    with grief and despair !
And the words, like the swift-flying balls, stung
    my ears as they passed to my breast,
Where the wounds that they made, wife, will
    linger till you and I take our long rest.

" My Elsie ! my own darling Elsie ! 'Twas here
    that thou gav'st me thy troth,
'Twas here thou didst kiss me to seal it ; 'twas
    here hand in hand we swore both,
To say not a word of the matter till I came
    back from over the sea,
O God ! if it could be Thy will that now I could
    die, blessing thee ! "

And there like a heap of dark shadows I found
    him all prone as he lay;
And I put my hand lightly upon him, and
    hoarsely said, " Lad, go away !
'Thou'rt not the first man who's been duped and
    befooled—ay, befooled by a smile ;
And the time may come surely around, thou'lt be
    glad thou hast suffered awhile.

" But that the woman who 'guiled thee should
    ha' been our young Elsie, far lief
I had seen her laid low i' the churchyard, ere *she*
    had brought thee to this grief ! "
Then he sprang to his feet with a bound, and
    firmly his hand grasped my arm.
" Peace ! " cried he.   " Peace ! not a word that
    can hurt her or do her a harm !

" She was always ' Our Elsie,' and I swore to be
    loving and true till the death ;
And thou art the father who reared her, the father
    through whom she drew breath :
And I tell thee, and swear to thee truly, that
    sooner, far sooner, than she—
Our Elsie, our bright, smiling Elsie, should suffer
    reproaches for me,—

" I would walk with my torn heart all bleeding—
    all bleeding, and bear the great load
Of this moment for ever—for ever, nor pray for
    the end of the road.
Heaven bless thee ! Thou camest to seek me—
    to seek me ! O angel of God !
Thou didst open the floodgates of mercy, when
    thou foundest me low on the sod ! "

And the lad threw his strong arms about me,
    and wept as he lay on my breast :
" I am sorry to leave *thee*, dear father ; but still
    thou wilt say it is best.
And say nought to the women to vex them ; the
    women—the women have griefs
Of which we know little, we men, with our work
    and our many reliefs."

Yet the lad was not one to sit down in a corner,
    to idle and weep ;
If the lightning had *then* struck him down, he'd
    ha' smiled as he went to his sleep.
But whilst the blood beat in his veins, he must
    up and be doing ; and so
He was off by the morn, far away from the scene
    of his hopes and his woe.

I knew, yes, I knew why he went to the land of
the fever and swamp :
But God He had gotten some work that the lad
must still do in the camp.
And so he toiled on for the good cause, and won
him no little renown ;
But if he had married our Elsie, she'd ha' smiled
all his high thoughts adown.

And the Angel of Death found him working in
the midst of the harvest he'd sown,
With the sheaves standing thickly around him :
he knew every ear that had grown.
And the marks of the daysman were on him,
who, labouring early and late,
Paused not, although languid and weary, till his
Master called loud at the gate.

COLD, PROUD MARGARET.

" I've longed to tell thee many a day,
    As we have walked along,
That all my love hath passed away
    As the echo of a song.

" Though it be hard for thee to hear,
    'Tis hard for me to say:
It seems, in sooth, as if a year
    Had passed o'er me this day.

" If love had been a thing at will,
    Nor had it now been said;
Or could it live by *seeming* still,
    When all its life was dead.

" But love comes like th' unbidden wind,
 And like the wind departs ;
There is no miracle can bind
 Two wayward human hearts.

" But I will keep my troth plight yet,
 If there be cruel need."
Then up rose cold, proud Margaret.
 " Nay, but there is no need."

He bit his lip in sheer despite,
 And strode across the floor.
" Maiden, for thy frank speech this night
 I thank thee evermore."

Lightly he sprang adown the stair ;
 With light heart went he forth.
Had she him given words more fair,
 It had brought little worth.

She laid her head upon the sill,
　　She clasped her fingers tight ;
She listened to each footfall, till
　　No sound came thro' the night.

And then with form erect and tall,
　　And stern and rigid face,
She softly swept across the hall,
　　With slow and even pace.

She turned from the half-open door,
　　Where showed a ruddy flame ;
She shunned with shuddering the floor
　　Whence children's laughter came.

　　*　　　*　　　*　　　*　　　*

A scarce-stirred stream, upon whose side
　　The rugged alders grew,
Which on its bosom in springtide
　　Their happy catkins threw ;

When Love had had its transient day,
  Whilst April suns looked on ;
Before the crooked branches gray
  Their downy leaves did don.

She leant against an alder tree,
  Its boughs swept o'er her face.
She said, " There is no room for me
  In all this wide world's space."

She looked athwart the alder tree,
  Into the pool beneath.
" Thy sullen gloom suits well, " said she,
  " For one in love with death."

A little star, whose steady light,
  Had travelled ages on,
Looked down, and with a flicker bright
  Danced tenderly upon

The quiet pool, where milfoil fine
And bristly brook-rush met.
" Thou art a foolish star to shine !"
Said woful Margaret.

Within the thick-leafed bower near
She sat her down, and leant
A weary head, that seemed to sear
The twigs that backward bent.

A timid bird, whose growing nest
Was hid those leaves among,
Peeped out to see what creature prest
So heedlessly along.

It peered into that cold, set face,
And laid its tiny beak,
As if in pity, one short space
Upon that cold, pale cheek.

Whereat there rose a surging flush,
   A thrilling tremor deep.
"Go, silly bird," sighed Margaret.   "Tush!
   Nay, thou hast made me weep."

FAIR ATHENA: AN INVOCATION.

I.

Αἵ τε λιπαραὶ καὶ ἰοστέφανοι καὶ ἀοίδιμοι,
'Ελλάδος ἔρεισμα, κλειναὶ 'Αδᾶναι, δαιμόνιον πτολίεδρον.
                              Pindar. Διθυραμβοι.

FAIR Athena, in the glory of thy all-pervading
    light,
Whilst my veiling eyelids droop astonied at its
    radiance bright ;

II.

And thy Doric columns, flushing with a deeper
    golden dye
Than the ages give them, proudly upwards gaze
    into the sky ;—

III.

I, a weak and lonely pilgrim from a misty isle
  afar,
After days and nights of travel, come to hail thy
  morning star.

IV.

Through the long years murm'ring voices, ofttimes heard in dead of night,
Filmy phantasms of the dream-hour, lulling
  reason in their might,

V.

Whispered, " Thou shalt yet behold it, yet shalt
  near the ruined shrine,
Where thy child-thoughts dwelt in rapture, spell-
  ing out each mythic line.

VI.

I rejoice I had not seen thee manacled, a slave,
  abased,
Discrowned, from thy queenly brows the violet
  wreath plucked off, effaced,

VII.

Trodden in the dust, and of its blossoms crushed,
the purple stain

Dyed the mourning garments Hellas wore till thy
day came again.

VIII.

Not thy day of former triumphs, not thy day of
golden shields,

Hung on high as votive off'rings, thank-gifts for
victorious fields ;

IX.

Not the day of Io pæans echoing thro' the lucid
air,

As the chariot wheels ascending, clanged along
the marble stair,

X.

When thy temple gates flung open, welcomed in
the joyous throng,

Flushed with ardour, and heart throbbing at the
high heroic song.

XI.

Not thy day of special honour, when a robe of
  white and gold—
Broider'd with the cunning needle, rich device in
  every fold,

XII.

Broider'd by the youthful virgins of the noblest
  race and fame,
Borne along in grave procession, offered to thy
  sacred name ;

XIII.

Whilst the green bough bearers followed, who the
  shining olive bore,
And the young men crowned with millet, singing praises evermore ;

XIV.

And the strangers, men and matrons, who in sign
  of alien race,
Held small boats and water-vases, as they walked
  in solemn pace ;

XV.

And the basket-bearing maidens, and the men
with shield and spear,
All thy sons and all thy daughters, marching on
in holy fear ;

XVI.

When the prison doors were opened—when the
sad and captiv'd throng,
Coming forth with sorrows lightened, feebly joined
their grateful song ;

XVII.

And when crowns of gold were given those who
had served country well,
And were chanted hymns of Homer, with their
mighty rhythmic swell.

XVIII.

Time o'er these hath wav'd his pinions, time o'er
these hath set his seal ;
That which hath been, shall be never, as the
newer truths reveal.

XIX.

But thy beauty still abideth, and thine hands are
  free to weave
Once again those spells, which Nature, casting in
  thy lap, doth leave.

XX

And thy children, gath'ring round thee, joy to
  raise thy marble walls ;
Joy to rear the gilded pillars, of thy academic
  halls. `

XXI.

Long those sons—the faithful remnant—fleeing
  to the rocky hills,
Waited, handing down the history of their
  country's woes and ills—

XXII.

Down thro' many weary ages ; and the echoes
  of their song,
Reached thee as thou laidest shackled—bade
  thee rise, and yet be strong.

XXIII.

By their blood poured out like water, seven long
years of cruel strife,

By the hopes that cling around thee, in thy fresh
awakened life,

XXIV.

Put not on thy high plumed helmet, take not up
the sword and spear,

Thou in whose extended genius higher powers
than these appear.

XXV.

Whilst the jealous nations striving, holding iron-
clads and shell,

Are the last best civilizers, long to learn their
lesson well ;

XXVI.

Be not touched by all the specious glamour of
the martial strain,

Whilst thy villages are scattered, and thy children
toil in pain.

XXVII.

Look around upon thy vineyards, the scant herb-
age of thy fields,

Thou who knowest all the science, all the arts
that labour yields.

XXVIII.

Nor love-longing eyes for ever turn unto the
gorgeous pile,

Where the Christian bells are silent, where the
Moslem min'rets smile.

XXIX.

Now thou art a queen and crownèd, would'st
thou tempt the changeful Fates ?

Could Athena be a handmaid, waiting at the
golden gates ?

XXX.

All the great renown and glory, that from age to
age was told

To our fathers—which our children's children
shall in homage hold,

XXXI.

Circled round thee as thou satest on thy barren
    Attic rock,
Whence thy hardy sons defiant hurled back every
    tyrant shock.

XXXII.

Mistress of the sea, and ruler of the hearts and
    minds of men,
Unto whom the gods in whispers gave to know
    their wisdom then,

XXXIII.

Where wast thou and all thy teachings, when
    beneath the Eastern sway
Of imperial rule thy greatness frittered year by
    year away?

XXXIV.

Overlayers of show and tinsel, fine-spun thoughts
    of subtle brains,
Gold and perfumes, royal purple, day by day
    were forging chains.

XXXV.

Laws, decrees, and holy synods—fathers, councils,
    what avails?
When the inner voice is silent, oracle and prophet
    fails.

XXXVI.

Where the earth withouten travail giveth fruits,
    nor taketh count
With what measure she outmeteth from her
    never-failing fount,

XXXVII.

There her children love to slumber in the lap of
    fragrant ease,
And, of tyranny the victims, sink by luxury's
    disease.

XXXVIII.

Thrice to thee hath Love in wisdom spoken.
    Once, when long ago
Thou gavest to the old man hemlock, for his gift
    of how to know.

XXXIX.

And again, when on the hill-side near thy Parthenon, there came

One who dared all base contumely but to preach
the Holy Name ;

XL.

One who knew how rich endowments puffeth up
with vain conceits;

One who warred against the unfaith springing
from the heart's deceits.

XLI.

And the third—the latest lesson written in thy
blood and tears—

Was the chastening of anguish where oft highest
love appears.

XLII.

Though my heart doth swell with sorrow at the
memory of thy grief,

Yet the thought is strong within me, born of
hope and fair belief,

XLIII.

That thou wilt in quiet meekness wear the honours
    thou hast won,

And in place of Gorgon breastplate, wilt the
    mystic peplum don.

XLIV.

Working still for sacred freedom with a noble
    firm resolve,

It shall be thy sole endeavour problems yet un-
    tried to solve.

XLV.

The music of the tinkling sheep-bells floats adown
    the rifted rock,

As from noontide heats the black-browed shep-
    herd leads his docile flock.

XLVI.

And a dreamy sense of beauty silenceth all doubts
    and fears ;

And a changeful vision passeth, and a shifting
    scene appears.

XLVII.

And I see thy ships deep laden going to and fro
with ease,

Bearing heavy freights of produce o'er thy ever
purple seas ;

XLVIII.

And the fisher boats sun-gleaming, with their
bright red lateen sails,

Dancing merrily to harbour, where a crowd their
coming hails.

XLIX.

And I see the young oaks rising, and the thickset pines once more,

With the wide-armed shining beeches, gladdening
thy ev'ry shore.

L.

Every true son deeming rightly, he who plants a
tree does well ;

And that he is alien truly, who with wanton
hands doth fell.

LI.

For of old the august mother, hearing in her
sacred grove
Sound of axe in cruel spoiling, did the outrage
base reprove.

LII.

And I see the silver currents of thy thread-like
rivers swell,
Nourished by the growing wood-glades on each
mountain-side which dwell.

LIII.

Cometh thro' the air song-laden, gladding hymns
from grateful earth,
For the freshet streams which waken budding life
from Attic dearth.

LIV.

But the visions now are fading, dying in a golden
mist ;
Glow of joy, as now the sun-god rock and hill
hath warmly kist.

LV.

And I see the columns only, in their silent
grandeur lone ;
At their feet the regal agaves, blooming from
the rugged stone,

LVI.

Mute and eloquent of greatness each to other
witness bears ;
Each to other hath been speaking through the
centuries' long years.

WAITING.

WHAT do the rushes say,

      Gwendolen,

That ever your footsteps lead that way?

Do you not fear the damps that cling

To your trailing skirt and light-shod feet?

Go you to hear the bittern sing?

Has the water-coot a voice more sweet

Than the throstle that sings in your garden's

      close?

Or is it to gaze at the water-snake

Wriggling within the shallow lake?

Or to hold commune with the toad morose,

Whose glittering eyes will never blink

As it stares in your face as you kneel by the

      brink?

I

Blows not the air chill,

        Gwendolen ?

Does not the mist like a mantle fill

That lower space, as thick-dewed night

Draws its close veil o'er the marshy waste ;

When the sky hangs out no lantern to light

Your wavering foot, to guide its haste,

But, as in baptism, pours instead

Water-drops on your unhooded head ?

Wan grows your cheek,

        Gwendolen !

Do the thoughts of your heart go forth to seek

Love from hate, and truth from guile ?

You may linger long beside the stream,

With a sometime frown, or a sometime smile,

Though from the moon's deceptive gleam

Will lie a shadow on the grass,

Yet the black poplar's arms stoop low,

And beneath them will not pass

Footfalls where cold arums grow.

With waiting long are you not now full weary?

Is not the day-star pale? is not the night most
    dreary?

I hold my heart, my soul, in fee;

I wear my thoughts not on my sleeve

For daws to peck at. What to me

The rushes whisper, I receive;

The water-snake it fears me not;

There is a fellowship between;

It doth not curse its narrow lot,

Its skin by sunlight hath some sheen.

The gold-eyed toad hath borne the blame

Of centuries in its calm breast;

It hath no scoff for me, I tame

My nature by its patient gest.

The drops wrung from my heavy hair

Are weighed and counted as they fall.

Since that my cheek was praised as fair,

It boots not now the day recall.

Is the night dreary ?

Is all waiting weary ?

Where the black poplar casts a shade along

Comes yet no footstep ? Heed not ; I am
   strong.

SONG OF THE WORKERS.

BROTHERS, work with heart and zeal ;
  Guide the powers that are given
You to know, and use for weal.
  Brains of mighty ones have striven
Labour's hindrances t' anneal.

Be it woof, or warp, or wheel,
  Be it ploughing, sowing grain,
Be it work in brass or steel,
  There is glory to attain—
In the love of good and fair ;
  In the noble thoughts that scorn
Great by littleness t' impair,
  Glossing sleight of falsehood born ;

In the joy which is a ray
    From the great Creative Mind,
Which, unceasingly, alway
    Worketh in most perfect kind.

THE SNAPPED STRING.

WITHIN the children's ward, beside
A little bed, there stands
A strong man, who a puppet holds
In his broad nervous hands.

A merry puppet full of fun,
Obedient to the string,
That here and there, and up and down,
Head, arms, and legs will fling.

A puppet whose sole mission was
To gladden heart of child,
Yet who could gravely look upon
Its antics strange and wild?

And the strong man with lusty will
Tugged at the twisted string,
With eager eyes that watched intent
For some sign answering.

But on that little shrunken face
There came no transient smile ;
Nor in the eye one kindling look
Of wonder passed awhile.

"You see, he is my only one—
His mother, too, is dead ;
And it was I—just think of that—
Who brought him to this stead.

"Twas I who dropped the unseen spark
Which seared him as he slept !
He looked so pretty sleeping, I——"
The strong man stopped and wept.

Down his care-furrowed cheek there ran
Quick tears of scathing grief.
" If he would only laugh—just once,
It would be such relief!

" Ha! there's a famous leap! Just look!
Now for another bound!
This time, I'll give so sharp a pull
We'll make him turn right round!"

Snap went the string, and motionless
The puppet's stiff limbs hung ;
And from the bed a feeble cry
Of trembling laughter rung :

"Oh, father!" Then my hand I laid
Upon the strong man's arm ;
" Hush! see you not?" A finer cord
Had broken 'neath his charm.

A GOLDEN DREAM.

Young Maggie's in the garden's close,
  Where the ripe currants glow ;
And slender lither fingers those,
  Which quick their clusters throw

Within the osier woven round
  For ample fruitage meet,
Which stands upon the thickset ground
  And touches her light feet.

Her large straw hat is tilted o'er
  A forehead frank and fair,
Which, whilst thus shadow'd, leaves the more
  Her twisted hair-coils bare ;

And oft her eyes with longings fond
  Look straight athwart the sky,
Above the wicket gate beyond,
  To the cool pine wood by.

Some vivid thoughts within her smile,
  Yet stay her not, until
High up, a glistening jewelled pile,
  The fruits her basket fill.

Then, as a kid from tether loosed,
  Which, with gay joyous bound,
Springs from the spot where lately noosed,
  She flees th' enclosèd ground ;

And sitteth on the cone-strewn earth,
  And leans against a tree.
The scented pine grove wakes with breath
  Of sweetest minstrelsy.

And straight some hundred humming things
   With tiny nimble feet,
And rainbow pageantry of wings,
   Upon her muslin meet.

And Maggie's earnest eyes are lit
   With strange unwonted light,
Seeing the changing forms which flit
   Before her wond'ring sight.

The whilst, with list'ning ear intent,
   Shows forth th' unconscious thought
That each, from realm of fairy sent,
   To her a message brought.

Till slow the heavy eyelids stoop
   To kiss the glowing cheek ;
And the unclasping fingers droop
   Which scarlet cup-moss seek.

Then happy weary Maggie sleeps,
   Until, in loud recalls,
Her name throughout the pine wood sweeps
   And on her ear close falls ;

When, hasting to her side there speeds,
   A stalwart youth, and clear
His voice rings—" Maggie little heeds
   I've sought her far and near."

Then Maggie, raising high her head,
   Looks up with angry gleam.
" I wish thou hadst not come," she said,
   " To spoil my golden dream."

" What dream at noontide, Maggie dear,
   Brings this untoward strain,
That makes me almost say, I fear
   To have thee dream again ? "

"I may not tell thee : I but know
    I was a fairy queen ;
And that my glories all did go
    When thou didst come between."

"Dear Maggie, I will make for thee,
    That thou may'st dream always ;
And fairy queen for ever be,
    Workdays and holidays."

Said Maggie, "That is foolish jest,
    Unless thou'rt fairy king ;
But like to mate with like is best,
    So help me now to bring

"The basket in, for I must home
    At once to set the cream—
Yet am I sorry thou didst come
    To spoil my golden dream."

HER MOTHER'S FAREWELL
TO GALESWINTHA.*

" YET but a little further—yet awhile

Let me my arms about my child enfold.

Oh, say not there is many a weary mile

Homeward again to traverse ! Ye have told

Each morning of the steep and rocky way

That stretched before us, hoping I should fear

The double perils, double cares, that lay

Between, ere on returning we shall near

The palace of your king, my lord. Ah me !

Too swift the chariot wheels have rolled along ;

* Galeswintha, daughter of Athanagild, King of Spain, and
married to Helperik, King of the Franks, afterwards murdered
by him and Fredegonda.—"Chronique de Gregoire de Tours."

Too swiftly have ye urged them.   *Ye* would see
Again your daughters,—hear the low-voiced song
As they walk by the loom or card the wool ;
Ye long to feel again their slender arms
Woven around you, and their kisses cool
The fever of your brows.   My vague alarms
Ye are impatient of.   Bethink ye well,
I have no daughter when my horses' heads
Turn   thitherwards.   There, doth none other
    dwell ;
Where the broad chestnut thick-leaved branches
    spreads
My daughter walks no longer.   Can ye know
The love of mother for her maiden child ?
The anxious tremors in her heart that grow
Whilst with her smiling prettiness beguiled ;
As with the blossoming years her beauties
    bring
A cause for gladness and a cause for tears ?

Gladness is born of loveliness, as sing

The bards ; but cankering sorrow bred of fears.

Ye look at me with doubting.   Ye are men,

And what ye will ye do ; poor women *we*,

Whose will must bend to others, even when

A diadem is lent us.   Ah ! let be

All joy divorced from thought of diadem !

The wives who call you husbands still do dwell

'Mid their own land and kindred : not to them

The royal maiden's saddest trials fell,

When they the threshold of their sheltering home

Passed, never to return ; they saw you—knew

The life that lay before them.   Ye did come

To woo them, and from wooing loving grew.

Ah, misinterpret', hapless womanhood !

When golden bracelets are the fetters worn,

And diamonds the price of servitude,

With flatteries, a thin disguise for scorn !

Through the long ages ye have suffered long—

K

Suffered through ignorance, by your own selves
 slain,
To make the theme and triumph of a song ;—
Ignoble triumph bringing bitter pain !
Where liberty is not, slavish virtues prized,
Therefrom a creeping undergrowth is fed
Of little fawning sophistries, despised
Of souls, by Freedom's gentle hand yled.
My Galeswintha, heavy seems the cloud
That hangeth o'er thee! Though a queenly crown,
The homage of a people strong and proud
Is waiting thee, ah ! would to God that down
Upon thy bier I'd seen thee laid the day
They gave thee from me—on thy virgin brow
The wreath of purity. By thy grave alway
I had then sate, and wept—as I do now,
But with less sorrow. Every night and morn
The holy chant in full-toned swell would rise
And vestal nuns in grave procession go,

To pray for thy sweet soul in sweetest wise ;
As for the pure, the purest prayers do flow.
What sayest thou, child ?   That God is there as
    here ;
And where Christ's lore is thou art not forlorn,
Although the evil powers reappear,
That have been cast from their high place in scorn ?
God shield thee from all warfare with such ill,
For thou art all too meek.   Once more, farewell.
The sun is sinking on the distant hill ;
My warriors' looks beseech me.   It is well.
Long taking leave takes not the sting away
Of partings which no day of meeting know.
As Love by loving still is fed alway,
So saddest thoughts by sad communion grow.
Farewell ! Now urge, my warriors, urge the steed,
Press on the chariot wheels.   How slow is seen
The weary drag that clogs your utmost speed
Now I am no more mother, but your queen !

A CRETAN LEGEND.*

FROM THE CRETEID OF ANTONIADES.

" I GLORY in thy light, O golden sun !

Thy rays who borrowed from my spreading hair.

Why dost thou, then, endure clouds dark and dun

To come between me and thy radiance fair ?

Come back ! come back ! and gild the earth again,

Or I will be the day-star—I, alone ;

And thou be banished to the shadowy plain,

'Mong wretched ghosts to pale and glimmer on."

---

* The superstition of the healing waters, still prevalent in
many parts of Greece, is derived from a tradition of a girl
who, proud of her beauty, insulted the majesty of Apollo and
Diana, and was changed by the latter into a bird, whose ever-
falling tears are the source of streams possessing curative
properties for diseases, mental as well as physical.

Thus spake with unadvised, rash tongue the
    maid,
As she sat weaving ; and Apollo heard,
And at the moment on the girl had laid
His fiery darts consuming, but appeared
His sister, ruler of the midnight skies,
The goddess Dian. " Stay, O brother ! stay
Thy anger just ; this silly child despise.
I will beguile her with my silver ray,
And her inflated heart in mocking jest
I will possess with my majestic sway,
As though I were obeying her behest."

Then did she bid the starry host retire,
For, in her shining chariot, she alone
Would ride the heavens.   The unnumbered
    quire
Fell back before their queen, who then, full-
    orbed,

Uprose and flashed her glory over space.

The maiden, sitting by her loom absorbed,

Rich cloth of gold was weaving.   With sweet
     grace

She moved the combs ; her mellow voice in song

Had hushed the wild waves' roaring, which lay
     calm

In list'ning silence.   The gay dolphin throng

Heard with delight the sweet tones' honied balm,

And left the brine to nestle in the sand.

All round the fisher boats lay at their ease ;

The nets, unheeded, cast upon the strand ;

Their torches gleaming on the quiet seas.

Till, on a sudden leaving her bright car,

The goddess as a huntress doth appear,

And darkness stealeth near and spreadeth far.

The girl she stayed her weaving, without fear

She called on Dian.   " Shine again, fair moon

Lighten the grieving earth.   It may not stay

Thy longer tarrying.   Shine ! or I must soon

Give my own radiance, make my own bright
    day."

Swift came whom thus invoked, in judgment
    came,

And on the maid poured down her vengeful
    scorn,

That ever after, steeped in sorrowing shame,

She waileth as a bird her state forlorn ;

And ever after weepeth hot sad tears—

Tears for her beauty lost, and all the joy

That comes from youth, which brighter now
    appears

Through all the goads which memories employ,

When reaping showeth duly what was sown.

So this poor bird from ever-welling tears,

Gives waters healing every sorrow known,

Each wearing grief that on the earth appears,

And soothes all other anguish save its own.

Such is the tale that on the Cretan isle

Still finds a credence in some simple breast,

Longing to meet that fountain's crystal smile

Which should its pain assuage, its woe arrest.

CRETAN HARVEST SONG.

FROM THE CRETEID OF ANTONIOS
ANTONIADES.

"Ἄσματα ψάλλουν τὸ βάρος τοῦ ἔργου κουφίζοντα καπως

Νέοι καὶ νέαι τοιαῦτα δὲ στίχοι δηλοῦοι δημώδεις."

Κρητηΐς.

NEAR where the thickset stubble stands
 Upon the sun-burnt plain,
Fifty and two right noble men
 Winnow the golden grain ;
Each one of the fifty-two
 Is strong in arm and tall,
But he that goes the foremost
 Is the strongest of them all.
The mother looks forth from her door,

A mother most discreet,
And sees her daughter going forth,
  The winnowers to meet.
" Oh, come from thence, my child ! " she cries,
  With anger in her tone.
" A tender maiden such as thou
  Must not go forth alone,
Lest that a dog might bite thee,
  Or raven with its beak
And cruel claw might tear away
  The roses from thy cheek ;
Or lest thy lily brow the sun
  With deepest brown might stain."
" No, mother, no ; I will not come,
  But here will I remain.
I take no heed if dogs should bite,
  Or if wild ravens tear ;
And if the sun do burn me black,
  I do not greatly care :

But I will for my husband take,
  The first man winnowing there."
" He, daughter ! he a dowry large
  Will ask, and we are poor :
We labour each day hard to live,
  Nor can increase our store."
" O mother ! give him promises—
  Yes, promises, no more.
Say that your goats are numerous
  As stars in midnight fair ;
But that for wealth in linen fine
  The heavens can't compare ;
For that of garments laid in press,
  As many I shall bring
As pebbles by the sandy shore,
  Or roses in the spring."

RHIGAS,*

HELLENIC POET AND PATRIOT.

RHIGAS ! thou soul of patriotic song !
Thou flame of freedom, with poetic fire
Sowing the seeds in soil which fallow long
Lay waiting, till thy blood the germs inspire
To wake to life.   Ha ! did proud Austria think,
When she did give thee to that Power—which
    still
Is as a festering sore—that she could blink
The heavy cloud that boded her fresh ill ?
Will Tyranny ne'er learn to mend its ways,
Until brought low and humbled in the dust ?

* Rhigas, a native of Thessaly, delivered up by Austria to
Turkey, was executed in 1798.

Had Tell not taught how man who dares, repays
At last, though bearing long the oppressor's
    lust ?—
That yet again, and yet again the greed
Of stern dominion leadeth her astray ?
The brave Pole saved her once, and for his meed,
When meted out was his heroic day,
With other spoilers she ne'er shamed to part
The garment he had worn with noble pride—
His country, which had lain so near his heart—
Rending it into portions to divide.
Time, it is true, reverses all.   Not now
The conquering crescent glitters at her gates :
The Gallic eagle, swooping down below,
Is threatening, and O irony of Fate !
Again she trembles, and she gives a sop
Unto that whilom foe, and Rhigas dies.
But count a patriot's blood out drop by drop ;
For each that falls a patriot will rise.

And Rhigas died, but not his songs, which, sung
On many a mountain-top mid crag and snows,
'Cross rocky chasms calls to freedom rung,
With stifled echoes from the plains below.
But as low whistling winds a storm presage,
Which, long held back, at last with sudden roar
Burst forth impetuous with a sudden rage,
Because of some restraining force before,—
So the low murmurs of a people swept
O'er isles, and hills, and mountain pass, and vale
Louder and louder chords discordant leapt
From earth till one blent chorus did prevail,
And " Liberty or Death ! " defiance hurled.
And one full joy to the high heavens rung,
When on the heights the holy flag unfurled,
Whilst the Great Feast the glad priests, blessing
    sung.
The mothers gave their sons with hearts aglow—
The mothers who had trembled with sad fears

When it was whispered them the breath below,

" Thou hast a man-child borne; " and when hot
    tears

Dropped on it as they swathed it round, aghast,

Lest that their blood had nourished day by day,

Fed by their breasts' sweet innocent repast,

A tool for their dread foe ; which smiling lay

Folded within their arms, whilst they used count

The chances, adding superstition's charms

(Made credulous by anguish), and amount

Of speculation make, to soothe alarms

With the fond selfish hope, " Not he, not he ;

The lot will miss my darling : it will fall

This time upon my sister's child, for she

Makes not the holy sign when night-birds call."

The bashful maidens laid their spinning down,

And cut their long hair short above the brow,

Whilst putting off the modest veil and gown

To fight as men with fathers, brothers, now.*

Thy song it was, O Rhigas! through the night—

The long, dark night of struggle, cheered them on;

Thy song it was, O Rhigas! by whose might—

Th' unequal war was waged, the victory won.

The pitying nations its far echoes•heard,

And the bright son of Albion awoke

From dreams of pleasure, by its cadence stirred,

And with a burst of hero's ardour broke

From bonds that held him, and he gave his life,

Ennobling thus himself for Hellas' sake.

Such the foundation stones in that good strife

For *her* rebuilding.   Such alone will make

A country ; poet ! hero ! and what more ?

A patriot ? Yes, a patriot. Yet that name

Standeth polluted now my sight before,

With deeds of violence and acts of shame.

---

* Ἱστορία τῆς Ἑλληνικῆς Ἐπαναστάσεως ὑπὸ Σ. Τρικούπη.

Who is a patriot ? Who ? Not one who hides

In darkness, and will slay a sleeping man,

Or maim the harmless creature that abides

Within the fold at nightfall.   Acts we scan

With the cause which prompteth.

     The ignoble deed

That cannot bear the open light of day,

Is of the old self-tainted tyrant breed,

Masked with a name—a country's peace to slay

No name so holy but has borne the stain

Of vile men's handling, 'bove all others high

That one—the patriot's, which again, again,

Trailing through filth, dares talk of freedom nigh

Rhigas *thy* hands were pure, *thy* cause was just ;

And through thy poet heart, thy Hellas freed,

Will ever think upon thy scattered dust ;

Her grateful love thy tomb, her liberty thy meed

L

SONNETS.

I.

THERE is a depth of quiet in the wood ;
Though the brown leaves are heaping on the
    ground,
A kind of hushing pause is breathed around,
As if it held a listening, prayerful mood.
Though trees bear signs of many a summer storm,
And clasping ivy prostrate lieth low,
Yet o'er their scars a gentle wind doth blow,
With loving pity kissing each bruised form.
O autumn breeze ! that sings blithe lullaby
To drowsy Nature, wooing it to sleep ;
O autumn leaves ! that drop so tenderly,
As if ye knew what charge ye had in keep,
Your voices have a sadness, but no sorrow,
Your " Good-night " whispers " Yet will come
    a morrow."

II.

SONNET.

To be beloved, we only need to die.
O beauteous Death ! that giveth us this boon.
However long our hearts in bondage lie,
Love in its warm embrace will hold us soon ;
And they who know us not, or know us wrong
Will by degrees come nearer to our side—
Will see the things that unto us belong,
And, as the shadowing veil is drawn aside,
Will note some fairness where they saw a stain,
Will strive each tone and accent to recall,
And with a sudden tenderness will strain
Love-longing eyes, now hoping to know all.
Were this thy only gift, this would be why,
O beauteous Death ! methinks, 'tis well to die.

III.

SONNET.

My child feet wandered in a mystic maze
Of dreams and fancies.   Gnomes and fairies
      danced
Around me in my rambles lone, entranced
With visions of my own ; for to my gaze
There was no beauty lent of earth or sky,
But in the very poverty around
Of Nature's riches, was my guerdon found ;
For smallest things were glories to my eye.
A gilded beetle found, though maimed and slain,
A growing pea to one small vase assigned,
A butterfly's rare fluttering on the pane,
Came fraught with novel beauty to my mind.
So now, though gardened round yet looking back
I feel not that my child life knew its lack.

IV.

SONNET.

THEY know not my heart's needs who still will
    chide
Because my feet seek not the busy throng ;
Nor the great peace that ever doth abide
Within the soul that finds its rest among
The perfect ways of Nature—who hath joy
In every tiny spiral that unfolds,
In the fringed chalice of the seeming toy
For fairies' use, which the gemmed wall-moss
    holds.
If the wild storms of passion or of grief
Leave me not scatheless as they onward sweep,
Shaking the boughs of life, and making brief
Some twining fancies that had rooted deep,
One true strong love, increasing with the years,
Filleth all gaps, nor leaveth room for tears.

V.

SONNET.

'TIS said that as the soul its goal draws nigh
The years are spanned, and o'er the bridge of
    Time
The farther side long left in childhood's prime
Is then the one most present to the eye.
And as of late I watched the ebbing flow
Of life in those dear ones now passed away,
I heard them murmur of a far-off day,
When parents' kisses set their hearts aglow.
So now, what means it that my morning dreams
Come floating back in rainbow-tinted light,
And all the landscape has the reflex bright
Of skies at dawning?   Are these sunset gleams,
That with the sparkle of the opening ray
Gild the horizon of a closing day?

VI.

SONNET.

" WHEN thou art rich in love, then fear thou most,
Nor boast of all thy wealth in flowering time ;
Look not too far ahead, and count the host
Of fruits from blossoms wanton in their prime.
Thou'lt find thy ruddiest apple at the core
Has nursed a maggot, making there its home,
And leaving it to sad decay before
The gathering-in of harvest-time has come."
God shield us all from such a cank'rous blight
As misbelief in promise of the spring.
Though cold winds tear the young buds in our
      sight,
The birds within some other boughs will sing.
Is our love bruised ?   Beware, for Love's dear
      need,
Lest at our heart's sound core the maggot mis-
      trust feed.

VII.

SONNET.

"WHAT is this bubble breath that men call
    Love—
This flower of phantasy with bloom so frail,
That bears no frost o' nights nor heats above ?
Howe'er it gaily hangs the fruit may fail ;
All must be summer shine, and dainty air,
And careful tending, and unwearied toil,
Or lost the hope of fond repayment fair ;
One gust will just suffice to mar and spoil."
Ay, if one love with hope of love returning,
Ay, if one measure heart-gifts like the rest,
Be sure light weight will set thy heart a-burning
At paltry change for gold coin of the best.
"So much for so much" is the huckster's thought ;
Divinest love it weighs and measures nought.

VIII.

SONNET.

As sings the lark in heaven without a care,
If it be heard, of Gods or men, but sings
From lustiness of heart, all unaware,
And to the listener thousand heart-throbs brings
So should the poet sing, nor thought of meed
Clog the winged thoughts that to the sky cærule
Should rise without a let, obeying need
None other than the universal rule,
That biddeth all things follow one behest—
To use unto the uttermost the power
To them assigned; to be not good, but best,
By being what their inmost needs empow'r;
If with such being there is no alloy,
No self to mar the perfect work of joy.

THINKING OF ATHENS.

THE asphodel, and not the violet,
Appealeth to my heart, Athenæ fair,
As thine own flower ; the asphodel, which yet
Its many-bloomèd spikes throws up i' the air,
Whilst deep down in the earth its roots are set.
Frail are its pale streak'd petals, which each breath
Of wind makes tremulous, and which too soon
Flutter away as if in love with death
Right joyously. Their beauty is a boon
For a day's disport, but there lies beneath,
A firm strong nature planted in a rock,
That bears with equal calm the heats and wind,
And showeth green, enduring every shock,
And giveth fruit according to its kind.

X.

IDLE HOURS: AT ATHENS.

THE purpled heights of Hymettus beneath,
On a May morning ere the sun be high,
With not a sound but that of Nature's breath,
With not one human form seen far or nigh,
How speed the hours, with Egina's blue sea
Skirting the distance, dotted with white sails !
I turn not now Athenæ's shrines to see ;
The present o'er this careless mood prevails.
Only to lie upon the violet slopes,
Only to fill the hands with thymy bloom,
Only to watch the beetle wise, which gropes
Its backward toilsome way to seek some home
Its rolling load to bury.   If this is idling clear
Then in such idling noon comes quickly near.

THE SAME.

THE Parthenon possessed me yesterday,
Athenæ ! and my brain was all involved,
With learned queries, till there came my way
A silky-coated sheep, who straightway solved
For that time all archaic studies.   She—
The pet companion of the warder there—
Bounded o'er prostrate carvings light and free,
Leapt up and down each wondrous marble stair ;
And ever laid she most caressingly
Her soft nose 'gainst my hand, and seemed to
    plead
For living Nature's sympathetic need,
And won her cause, striving unceasingly,
That side by side we passed an hour alone,
I sitting, she reclining, on the time-worn, rugged
    stone.

THE AKROPOLIS OWL.

THE nightingale sings in the royal close,
Where amaranths are carpeting the ground ;
Although it doth not woo the musky rose,
Whose fragrant canopies with buds abound,
But hath its faithful partner nesting near
The splashing fountains, or the freshet green.
The garden is a sanctuary ; fear
Mars not the joy which goes their love between
But on the rough Akropolis alone,
The speckled-breasted owl hath still its home,
Making the ruined Parthenon its own,
Where nightly with soft winging it doth roam
In freedom, yet in danger, and its cry
In shrilly sadness 'plains for memories gone by

XIII.

ON THE BRINGING INTO ATHENS THE BODY OF MR. OGLE.

FOR what the wail of sorrow heard to-day
Throughout fair Athens, who with veiled brow
Sheddeth hot tears ?   Along the darkened way
Why wait her downcast sons in silent row,
With arms reversed ?   Sleeps, then, her young
    crowned king
In death ?   For here a nation's deep grief shows ;
Happy dies he whose dying love doth bring !
Regret so deep for monarch seldom flows.
What say the weeping women ?   'Tis not *he*,
Our king, he mourneth with us.   Hellas land
Nor gave him birth, love only, love ! which we
In kisses long to shower on his cold hand—
The fair-haired, frank-browed Englishman who
    came
With burning heart for truth and right aflame."

XIV.

SONNET.

νῦν δ' ἐφίητι τὼ τὠργείου φυλάξαι
ῥῆμ' ἀλαδείας ὁδῶν ἄρχιστα βαῖνον,
χρήματα, χρήματ' ἀνήρ, ὃς φᾷ κτεάνων θαμὰ
λειφθεὶς καὶ φίλων.—Ἰσθμίαι Π. i.

THE Argive's saying will our hearts but sear
If we do heed it—"Wealth doth make the man."
It makes or it unmakes him.   Oh, come near,
Come nearer to us that we may ye scan,
Ye powers, that veil your eyes when love of gold
Creeps on our chilling hearts !   Doth then the
     Muse,
As by the thrilling words of Pindar told
Long years ago, her sweet-toned lyre refuse
Unless with gold or silver overlaid ?
Nor then as now, nor now as then, was fire
Ere kindled by the gods for bounties paid.
Deeds can alone the high-toned theme inspire ;
And where these are not, song, with flapping
     wings,
Or gold-clogged, or earth-soiled, to earth yet
     clings.

XV.

AFTER PINDAR.

γνῶθι νῦν τὰν Οἰδιπόδα σοφίαν. εἰ γάρ τις ὄζους ὀξυτόμῳ πελέκει
ἐξερείψαι κεν μεγάλας δρυός, αἰσχύνοι δέ οἱ θαητὸν εἶδος·
καὶ φθινόκαρπος ἐοῖσα διδοῖ ψᾶφον περ' αὐτᾶς,
εἴ ποτε χειμέριον πῦρ ἐξίκηται λοίσθιον·
ἢ σὺν ὀρθαῖς κιόνεσσιν δεσποσύναισιν ἐρειδομένα
μόχθον ἄλλοις ἀμφέπει δύστανον ἐν τείχεσιν, ἑὸν ἐρημώσαισα χῶρον.
Πυδια iv.

As when some cruel hand unawed, and bold,
Has dared with ruthless axe to lop and mar
The grandeur of an oak in forest old,
And fells its spreading arms, and many a scar
On its broad trunk in bleeding witness leaves,
And triumphs in the spoils he bears away ;
The shapeless logs which on the fire he heaves,
When winter winds blow chill and skies look
      gray,
Will yet, in burning, their proud birth avow.
The stately carvèd columns which uprise,
To bear up the high roof in double row
On some far shore, mayhap 'neath alien skies,
Though from their forest home and parent torn,
Will still assert of what high lineage born.

XVI.

KENTISH HEDGEROWS IN AUTUMN.

THROUGHOUT the world is there a scene more
      fair,
After its kind, than Kentish hedgerows, seen
In autumn days, before a frosty air
Has frolicked in and out their bowery green ?
The wealth of gold and crimson shows as gay
As summer flowers on the cornell's bough ;
The high dark pine a crown with ruddy ray
From woodbine's clustering berries weareth
      now.
Whilst bryony, with purpled heart-shaped leaves,
From right to left contrariwise doth twine,
Laughing in glorious freedom as it wreathes
And hangs gay bunches, which will glow and
      shine
For thee and me, my love, upon our wall,
Till spring-time come, nor will one berry fall.

M

ON A MONUMENT BY CHAN-TRY, IN CHEVENING CHURCH, KENT.

COLD is the pure white marble, and quite cold
The graceful form that seems in sleep to breathe,
And with a smile of sweet content doth fold
One lovely arm a little babe beneath ;
The infant of an hour, to her fond breast
Which nestling, eloquent of joy, lies pressed.
No wonder he, with heart o'ercharged by grief
When first he gazed thereon, gazed yet again ;
Nor with the gazing felt one short relief,
But evermore increased the bitter pain
Of loss beyond retrieve, which that carved stone
In all its sculptured art so vivid made,
That tortured Love shook Reason from its throne,
Hasting to seek thro' death that tomb's lov'd
        shade.

GUILDHALL PIGEONS.

WHERE, 'mid the city turmoil and the throng,
A crowd of peaceful doves do haunt the way
Before the seat of justice ; them among
A full hour long I stood one autumn day,
And wove a fond imagining, as dream
Secluded men full wrongly oft.   How sweet
The mission of those graceful birds did seem !
What blissful lessons hovered near their feet !
When suddenly there came a wretched train
Of men, of boys, of girls, who with stern haste,
As foes to order, and a moral stain,
Were borne to punishment, for their lives' waste.
They passed, and then the doves came as before,
And, cooing, picked the scattered crumbs once
    more.

XIX.

SONNET.

O DEPTHS of love! deep down in human hearts
Why do ye linger till Death's curfew tolls
A warning that the day of Life departs,
And the stern march its muffled summons rolls?
Still like the hidden spring beneath our feet
Ye wait, until a power not your own
Pierces the rock, when upward boundeth fleet
The silvery waters freed, no more alone,
They pour their blessings on the thirsty ground,
That for their freshening wearied had and
  yearned ;
Yet where a never-failing stream is found,
The earth gives of its best, as rightful earned,
And giveth with great joy, as if to say,
There is no love that Love will not repay.

IN THE EVENING.

LOOK yonder, love, above the elm tree's bough
The western star is peeping.   It is now
A year since I began to rhyme to thee,
In answer to our souls' deep mutual need.
A very little thing will ofttimes speed
The wished-for end, when larger methods flee :
A word, a smile, will lift a heavy load,
Where deepest reason with its logic fails ;
One stumbles from a pebble in the road,
Who safely through the stormy ocean sails.
O Hesperus ! O Love ! give still sweet light,
Our earth-rays taking back to gild thy night !

II.

For love that gives, and love that takes
        sweet :
In mutual needs do mutual blessings meet.

And thus it is we feel a fuller joy,
When standing hand in hand as we do now,
With mystic sense of beauty filled ; whilst thou,
Light-following Hesperus ! our thoughts employ,
By thinking this dim earth on which we stand
Is unto thee a glory and a shine
Above all others in Night's circling band,
When thou art lost to us with Eve's decline ;
And that perchance from lovers, poets, rise
Our orb's glad welcome to thy midnight skies.

PRINTED BY WILLIAM CLOWES AND SONS, LIMITED,
LONDON AND BECCLES.

www.ingramcontent.com/pod-product-compliance
Lightning Source LLC
Chambersburg PA
CBHW020005030726
47500CB00002B/452